The King Who Rained

by FRED GWYNNE

Simon and Schuster Books for Young Readers
Published by Simon & Schuster Inc., New York

Copyright © 1970 by Fred Gwynne

All rights reserved including the right of reproduction in whole or in part in any form.

Published by Simon and Schuster Books for Young Readers, A Division of Simon & Schuster, Inc.

Simon & Schuster Building Rockefeller Center

1230 Avenue of the Americas New York, NY 10020

Originally published by Windmill Books, Inc. and Simon & Schuster, Inc.

Simon and Schuster Books for Young Readers is a trademark of Simon & Schuster, Inc.

Manufactured in the United States of America

10 9 8 7 6 5 4

10 9 8 7   pbk

Library of Congress Cataloging in Publication Data

Gwynne, Fred.

   The king who rained.

   SUMMARY: A little girl pictures the things her parents talk about, such as a king who rained, bear feet, and the foot prince in the snow.

   1. English language—Homonyms—Juvenile literature.   [1. English language—Homonyms]   I. Title.

PE1595.G75 1980   428.1   80-12939

ISBN 0-671-66363-1

ISBN 0-671-66744-0 (pbk.)

Daddy says there was a king
who rained for forty years.

there are forks in the road.

Daddy says
he has a mole
on his nose.

lambs gamble on the lawn.

Sometimes
Mommy says
she has a frog
in her throat.

Other times she says she's
a little horse and
needs the throat spray.

And when I give it to her,
she says I'm a little deer.

My big sister's getting married
and she says I can hold up her train.

Daddy says next time he paints the house he's going to give it two coats.

Daddy says there's
a head on his beer.

Daddy says all we get
in the mail are big bills.

Mommy says not to bother

her when she's playing bridge.

Daddy says our family
has a coat of arms.

Daddy says we should
live in the present.

Mommy says little children
always have bear feet.

I've heard Daddy talk about
the foot prince in the snow…

...and the blue prince for
the new room on our house.

Daddy says some boars
are coming to dinner.

Did you ever hear
such a bunch
of fairy tails?